ENID BLYTON LIBRARY

Titles in this Series

The Little Button Elves
Hoo Hoo's Party
My Nut I Think!
Pipes for Old Puff
What! No Cheese!
The Wizard's Needle

ISBN 0 86163 097 1

First published as *Nature Tales*
by W. & A.K. Johnston and G.W. Bacon Limited, 1948
This edition first published 1985
Second impression 1986

Published by Award Publications Limited, Spring House,
Spring Place, London NW5 3BH, England

Printed in Belgium

Pipes for Old Puff

& The Little Down Cushion

Illustrated by RENE CLOKE

AWARD PUBLICATIONS

PIPES FOR OLD PUFF

PUFF, the old gnome, sat down at the foot of the big oak tree in spring and lit his pipe.

Puff wasn't much bigger than a daisy, so, as you can guess, his pipe was very small and not much smoke came from it.

But there was quite enough to annoy a caterpillar eating a leaf. He called down to Puff. "Hey, you! Go away at once! I don't like your smell."

Puff looked up
indignantly. "My smell,
indeed!
It's my pipe you
can smell, and
a very nice smell
it makes too.

Cheeky young caterpillar, talking to me like that!"

The oak tree spoke next. It had a queer whispering voice, like the voice of all its leaves together.

"Puff, is that you? These caterpillars will kill me! Each year there are more and more of them, eating my young leaves. Smoke your pipe as much as you can, up in my branches. Perhaps you will make the caterpillars leave me and then my leaves can grow in peace."

So Puff took his little pipe up into the oak tree and smoked it there. All the caterpillars crawled away from the smoke but they went to another part of the tree. So his smoke wasn't much good.

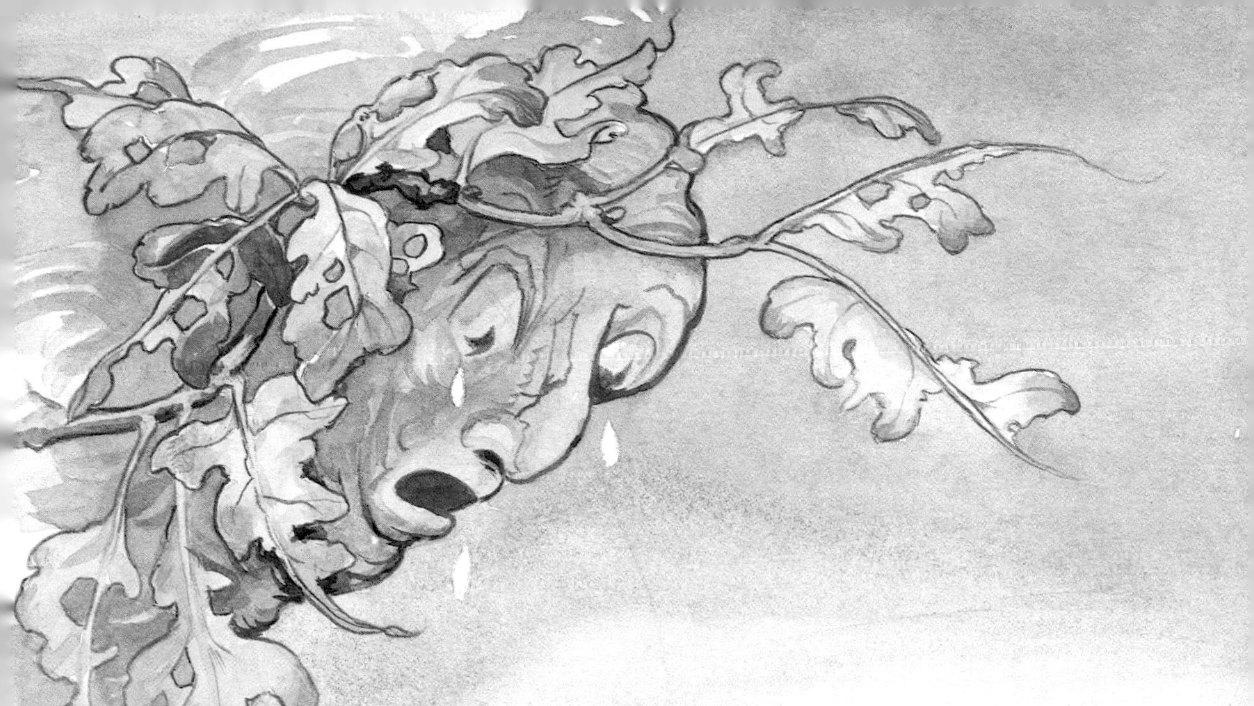

More and more caterpillars hatched out of eggs in the oak tree, and soon the poor tree began to look dreadful. Some of the twigs were quite bare, for all the leaves had been eaten.

"I shall die," said the oak tree. "I need my leaves to breathe with. I shall die."

Puff didn't like the rude, greedy caterpillars. Two of them actually ran off
with his pipe one day and pushed it down
an owl's hole in the tree!, so that he couldn't
smoke any more.

He went to see his friends the robins,
who had a nest full of hungry young ones
down in the ditch.

"Robin," he said to the mother bird, who was just giving her nestlings some caterpillars she had found.

"Robin, come with me! I will show you where there are caterpillars without number for you to feed your hungry babies on!"

When the two robins saw the fat little caterpillars, chewing at the oak leaves by the hundred, they were full of delight. Now it would be easy to feed their young ones.

So, day after day, they visited the oak tree and filled their beaks with the wriggling caterpillars. They took hundreds and hundreds of them, and soon the oak tree felt that it was safe to grow more new young leaves.

It was very grateful to the old gnome. "I'm sorry you've lost your pipe, Puff," said the tree, in it's whispery voice. "Very sorry indeed. I know how fond of a smoke you are. Come back in the autumn, will you-say the end of September-and I'll see what I can do for you!"

So Puff came back in the autumn and looked up at the big oak tree. It had many acorns on the twigs now, smooth and oval.

The wind blew and some of them tumbled down from their cups.

They left their empty cups on the tree.

Puff stared at them in delight.

"Why, you've put your acorns into pipes!" he cried. "Pipes, pipes, hundreds of pipes-and all so beautifully carved round the bowl, too. Thank you, oak tree, I'll help myself and enjoy a really good smoke."

So he did and you should have seen him puffing away.

Do you want to see the pipes he used? Well, go to the oak tree and have a look at the acorns there. They are all growing in Puff's little pipes!

THE LITTLE DOWN CUSHION

TIPPITTY the elf was stuffing a cushion with thistledown. It was to be a present for her Aunt Big-Eyes. "She'll like it," thought Tippitty. "It will be so very very soft! She'll fall asleep as soon as she puts her head on my little down cushion."

Tippitty had taken the thistledown from the thistle heads at the edge of the common.

There was a big patch of them there and the purple heads had turned to grey silky down, just right for cushions.

"I'll catch the four o'clock bus and go to Aunt Big-Eyes for tea," thought Tippitty. She finished stuffing the cushion and sewed it up neatly. Then, carrying it under her arm she set off for the bus.

But it didn't come. Tippitty wondered if her clock was wrong. She looked about for a dandelion clock to tell her the time. Ah, there was one!

She picked it and held it to her mouth to blow–just like you do when you want to tell dandelion time! Puff! One o'clock. Puff! Two o'clock. Puff! Three o'clock. Puff! Four. . . . Oh dear, oh dear, who was this coming along looking so angry?

It was Witch Frowner.
She caught hold of
Tippitty and shook her.
"You bad elf! Look what
you are doing! Blowing
those dandelion seeds over the wall into
my beautifully kept garden!"

"I was only telling the time," stammered poor Tippitty, frightened. She remembered that Witch Frowner had a most beautiful

garden, in which not one single weed was allowed to grow. Oh dear- and all the dandelion seeds had been floating over the wall!

Witch Frowner caught hold of the new little down cushion.

"You can give me this to make up for your naughtiness!" she said. "I'd like it for my garden chair!"

And, to Tippitty's horror, she went off with the new little cushion of down. Poor Tippitty! She ran off home, crying bitterly.

Witch Frowner took the cushion into her garden. She put it into her chair and laid her head on it. How soft it was! Serve Tippitty right for blowing seeds of weeds into her lovely garden!

Now, when the autumn came, Witch Frowner took her garden chair indoors. But the little cushion fell to the ground unnoticed and was left behind.

The rain came and wetted it.
A mouse nibbled
a hole in it.
All the thistledown
inside began
to leak out.

Now each bit of thistledown had a tiny seed belonging to it. The down flew here and there over the garden, taking the seeds with it. They fell to earth and lay there waiting for the time to come to grow.

And when the spring came, what a shock for old Witch Frowner! Thistles sprang up all over her garden, in every nook and cranny.

"Who put them there?" raged the witch. And the thrush in the apple tree answered cheekily.

"You did, you did, you did!"

"You're a fibber!" cried the witch. But he wasn't – he was telling the truth, wasn't he?